FERDINANDUS
TAURUS

FERDINANDUS TAURUS

a Munro Leaf conscriptus
a Roberto Lawson depictus

Latine ab Elizabetha Hadas redditus

Ex Officina D. Godineana

BOSTONI

MM

This edition first published in 2000 by
David R. Godine, *Publisher, Inc.*
Post Office Box 450
Jaffrey, New Hampshire 03452
www.godine.com

Originally published in 1962 by David McKay Co., Inc.
Translation copyright ©2000 by the Estate of Elizabeth C. Hadas

Originally published in English as *The Story of Ferdinand*
Copyright 1936 by Munro Leaf and Robert Lawson
Copyright © renewed 1964 by Munro Leaf and John W. Boyd

"On *Ferdinandus Taurus*" copyright ©2000 by Rachel Hadas
"Translating the Vast World" copyright ©2000 by Elizabeth C. Hadas

LIBRARY OF CONGRESS CONTROL NUMBER 00 134966
ISBN 1-56792-127-2

Third printing, 2014
PRINTED IN CANADA

Meo marito
sine quo
fieri non potuisset

Olim in Hispania

erat taurulus nomine
Ferdinandus.

Alii tauruli omnes quibuscum
habitabat currebant et
exsultabant et cornibus alius
alium petebant,

sed minime Ferdinandus.

RL

Tranquille sedere et flores olfacere malebat.

RL

Diligebat locum quendam in prato sub querco corticea.

Sub grata umbra huius arboris, quae erat ei dilectissima, totos dies sedebat et florum odoribus se delectabat.

Mater Ferdinandi, quae erat vacca, interdum angebatur, verita ne solitarius sine amicis esset.

"Cur," inquit, "non vis currere et cum aliis taurulis ludere et exsultare et caput tundere?"

Abnuit tamen Ferdinandus. "Malo," inquit, "hic manere, ubi tranquille sedere et flores olfacere possum."

Parens filium non solitarium esse sensit, et quod erat mater sagax, etsi vacca, eum ibi modo sedere et laetum esse sinebat.

Annis labentibus Ferdinandus crescebat atque maximus et validus fiebat.

Alii tauri omnes qui in eodem prato cum illo creverant, totos dies inter se pugnabant. Capita alius alium contundebant et cornibus petebant. Deligi ad pugnandum in tauromachiis Madriti—id maxime cupiebant.

Sed minime Ferdinandus: malebat adhuc sub querco corticea sedere, nihil agens, et flores olfacere.

RL

Quodam die quinque homines
advenerunt, ridiculose
pilleati, ad taurum omnium
maximum, celerrimum,
ferocissimumque deligendum
qui in tauromachiis Madriti
pugnaret.

Tauri ceteri omnes
concursabant, anhelabant,
capita contundebant,
exsultabant exsiliebantque, ut
hominibus illis viderentur
validissimi acerrimique atque
maxime ad pugnam deligendi.

Cognoverat Ferdinandus
illos se numquam delecturos
esse, neque eum huius
paenitebat. Quare ad quercum
corticeam istam amabilem
profectus, illic subsedit.

Quo in loco tamen subsideret
non animadvertit: nam non in
gramine dulci umbrosoque
consedit, sed in ape
bombitante.

Tu si apis bombitans esses et taurus in te sederet, quid, quaeso, factura esses? Nempe istum pungeres. Quod profecto fecit apis illa.

Vah! Quam dolor! In altum exsiluit Ferdinandus, vehementer sufflans. Circumcurrebat, anhelabat, efflabat, capite minitabatur, solum pedibus pulsabat, sicut demens.

RL

Quae cum viderent quinque homines illi, laetabantur conclamaveruntque. Ecce taurus omnium taurorum maximus ferocissimusque, et ad pugnandum aptissimus!

Carro igitur eum abvexerunt
in tauromachiae diem.

MADRITUM

RL

Quam festa erat dies illa!

Vexilla aurae ventilabant,

tubae cornuaque canebant . . .

et mulieres omnes
pulcherrimae crines floribus
adornaverant.

Pompam in arenam duxerunt.

RL

Primo incesserunt pedites qui
Banderilleri appellantur,
stimulos gerentes longos
acutosque taeniis redimitos
quibus taurum pungerent
atque exacerbarent.

RL

Deinde invecti sunt equites
qui Picadores appellantur
equis ieiunis, hastas
praelongas gerentes quibus
taurum pungerent et maiore
etiam impetu exacerbarent.

RL

Ultimus incessit pugnator ipse, qui Matador appellatur, omnium superbissimus. Sibi videbatur bellissimus esse, et mulieribus se inclinabat. Pallio rubro indutus, gladium gerebat, quo taurum ultimus pungeret.

Postea incessit taurus. Scisne quis fuerit taurus iste?

—IPSE FERDINANDUS.

Ei nomen Ferdinandum Ferocem indiderunt. Timebant eum Banderilleri omnes, timebant Picadores, et ipse Matador timore rigebat.

Ad mediam arenam cucurrit
Ferdinandus. Conclamabant
omnes plaudebantque,
exspectantes Ferdinandum
acriter pugnaturum esse et
caput iactaturum et cum
strepitu sufflaturum et
cornibus minaturum.

RL

Ferdinando aliter visum. In mediam arenam progressus, floribus in mulierum pulcherrimarum crinibus visis, sedebat curis solutus et florum odoribus se delectabat.

RL

Nullo modo volebat pugnare vel ferocem se praebere, neque ullo modo poterant eum cogere. Sedebat tantum et odoribus se delectabat. Irascebantur Banderilleri, magis irascebantur Picadores, et tantopere irascebatur Matador ut lacrimaret quod nequisset se ostentare pallio indutum gerentemque gladium.

RL

Necessitati ergo obsecuti,
domum Ferdinandum
reportaverunt.

Quoad mihi notum est, adhuc tranquille sedet Ferdinandus sub querco illa corticea dilectissima, flores olfaciens.

Beatissimus est.

FINIS

Index Verborum

abnuo, -nuere, -nui, *refuse, shake one's head*

abveho, -ere, -vexi, -vectus, *carry off*

adhuc, still, *even now*

ago, -ere, egi, actus, *drive, do*

aliter, *otherwise*

alius, alia, aliud, *another*

angor, angi, *feel distress, worry*

anhelo, -are, -avi, -atus, *puff, snort*

animadverto, -ere, -verti, -versus, *notice*

apis, apis, *f.*, bee; apis bombitans, *bumblebee*

aptus, -a, -um, *fit, suitable*

arbor, arboris, *f.*, *tree*

beatus, -a, -um, *happy, blessed*

bellus, -a, -um, *handsome, stylish*

cano, -ere, cecini, cantus, *sing, play (an instrument)*

caput, capitis, *n.*, *head*

celer, celeris, celere, *fast, swift*

concurso, -are, -avi, -atus, *run about*

contundo, -ere, -tudi, -tusus, *beat, strike*

cornu, corpus, *n.*, *horn*

cresco, -ere, crevi, cretus, *grow large, grow up*

crinis, crinis, *m.*, *hair*

cupio, -ere, cupivi, cupitus, *desire, wish*

curro, -ere, cucurri, cursurus, *run*

delecto, -are, -avi, -atus, *delight*

deligo, -ere, -legi, -lectus, *choose*

demens, dementis, *out of one's mind, crazy*

diligo, -ere, -lexi, -lectus, *love, value highly*
dolor, doloris, *m.*, *pain*
dulcis, dulce, *sweet*
ecce, *behold*
efflo, -are, -avi, -atus, *puff, snort*
etsi, *although*
exacerbo, -are, -avi, -atus, *irritate, provoke*
exsilio, -ire, -silui, *spring, leap*
exsulto, -are, -avi, -atus, *jump*
ferox, ferocis, *fierce*
fio, fieri, factus sum, *be made, become*
flos, floris, *m.*, *flower*
gramen, graminis, *n.*, *grass*
homo, hominis, *m.*, *man*
idem, eadem, idem, *the same*
ieiunus, -a, -um, *thin, spiritless*
illic, *there*
incedo, -ere, -cessi, -cessus, *walk, march*
inclino, -are, -avi, -atus, *bend, bow*
indo, -ere, -didi, -ditus, *give, apply to*
induo, -ere, -dui, -dutus, *put on*
inquit, *he (or she) says*
inveho, -ere, -vexi, -vectus, *carry in; (in passive), ride*
irascor, irasci, iratus, *grow angry*
labor, labi, lapsus, *glide, slip*
laetor, -ari, -atus, *be glad*
ludo, ludere, lusi, lusus, *play*
Madritum, -i, *n.*, *Madrid*
malo, malle, malui, *prefer*
mater, matris, *f.*, *mother*

minime, *not at all*

minitor, -ari, -atus, *threaten*

mulier, -ieris, *f., woman*

nempe, *certainly*

nequeo, -ire, -ivi, -itus, *be unable*

nihil, *nothing*

nomen, nominis, *n., name*

obsequor, -sequi, -secutus, *obey, yield to*

olfacio, -ere, -feci, -factus, *smell*

olim, *once upon a time*

omnis, omne, *all*

pallium, -i, *n., cloak*

paeniteo, -ere *(usually impersonal), be sorry*

pedes, peditis, *m., foot soldier*

peto, -ere, petivi, petitus, *seek, attack*

pilleatus, -a, -um, *hatted, wearing a hat*

pompa, -ae, *f., parade*

praebeo, -ere, praebui, -bitus, *offer; (reflexive), show oneself*

pratum, -i, *n., meadow*

profecto, *indeed, truly*

proficiscor, -cisci, profectus, *set out*

progredior, -gredi, -gressus, *go forward*

pulso, -are, -avi, -atus, *strike, beat*

pungo, -ere, pupugi, punctus, *prick, sting*

quaeso, -ere, *beg, ask*

quercus, -i, *f., oak tree;* quercus corticea, *cork tree*

quidam, quaedam, quoddam, *a certain*

quoad, *as far as*

redimio, -ire, -dimii, -dimitus, *wreathe round*

rigeo, -ere, *be stiff*
ruber, -bra, -brum, *red*
sagax, -acis, *understanding, wise*
scio, scire, scivi, scitus, *know*
sedeo, -ere, sedi, sessus, *sit*
sicut, *as, just as*
sino, -ere, sivi, situs, *allow, permit*
solitarius, -a, -um, *lonely*
solum, -i, *n., ground, earth*
solvo, -ere, solvi, solutus, *loosen, free*
stimulus, -i, *m., goad*
strepitus, -us, *m., noise*
subsido, -ere, -sedi, -sessus, *sit down*
sufflo, -are, -avi, -atus, *puff, blow*
taenia, -ae, *f., ribbon*
tantopere, *so much*
tantum, *only*
tauromachia, -ae, *f., bullfight (from the Greek)*
taurus, -i, *m., bull;* taurulus, *little bull*
tranquille, *quietly*
tundo, -ere, tutudi, tunsus, *beat, thump*
umbra, -ae, *f., shade*
umbrosus, -a, -um, *shady*
vacca, -ae, *f., cow*
validus, -a, -um, *strong*
ventilo, -are, -avi, -atus, *wave, blow*
vereor, -eri, veritus, *fear*
vexillum, -i, *n., flag*
volo, velle, volui, *wish*

ON FERDINANDUS TAURUS

Whenever I think about either *The Story of Ferdinand* or *Ferdinandus Taurus*, what come to mind first are Robert Lawson's wonderful illustrations. There are the cork trees loaded with tempting-looking bunches of corks hanging in graceful clusters; the fascinating patches on the men's clothes; the ladies' towering headdresses; the indignant eye of the bumblebee onto which Ferdinand is about to lower his bulk. Looking at the book this time around, I notice I see things in a maternal light: the eloquent gesture of Ferdinand's hoof when he is explaining to his mother *(mater sagax, etsi vacca)* that he prefers to sit quietly and smell the flowers; or the growth chart on the stump *(tres menses; unus annus; duo anni)* as Ferdinand matures from a calf into a bull.

In 1962, the year *Ferdinandus Taurus* was published by David McKay, I was fourteen. My sister Beth's and my growth chart was inside the door of the linen closet, at the end of the winding hall in our Riverside Drive apartment. My mother had then been teaching Latin at the Spence School for three or four years; having begun as a part-timer, she was probably working full-time by now. When had she found the time to translate *Ferdinand the Bull* into Latin? I don't know. When I think back to our family sitting after supper around the big dining room table (where Beth or I might be doing our homework in our rooms—that table was a magnet), I see my mother correcting her students' homework or writing report cards, not working on *Ferdinandus*. Nevertheless, the work got done. This unobtrusive presence of my mother, who never made heavy weather of any task, was, and remains, profoundly comforting; to be her child was to be taken care of.

I know that my father, Moses Hadas, helped her with the translation; the phrase "wearing funny hats" was a challenge to her, since Roman men did not wear hats, and it sticks with me that the solution *ridiculose pilleati* (like a pilleated woodpecker) was supplied by him. But only this time around do I note her dedication: *Meo marito sine quo fieri non potuisset.* Perhaps she was recalling that she and her future husband had met when she took his Latin prose composition course at Columbia Summer School.

Finally, there is the allegory of Ferdinand, the gentle noncombatant bull. His safe return, after he has gone on a sit-down strike in the bull ring, to the flowery meadows of his calfhood now seems to me to defy all probability. But it never bothered me when I was a child; after all, where, if not in a children's book, should a character deserve to live happily ever after? *Beatissimus est.*

I would like to thank Charles Martin, distinguished poet and translator of Catullus and Ovid, for suggesting, when he saw *Ferdinandus* on my bookshelf in May of 1998, that the book ought to be reprinted; David R. Godine, longtime friend and lover of books and of Latin, for his faith in the idea; and my sister, Beth Hadas, for doing most of the work toward making this new edition a reality. In reissuing the book, Beth and I are paying tribute to a loving mother who was indeed sagacious, and whose legacy Beth and I, my husband George, and my son Jonathan cherish. In addition, I hope the book will find its way into the hands of some of my mother's many Latin students at the Spence School—or rather, into the hands of their children.

—Rachel Hadas
New York, March 1999

TRANSLATING THE VAST WORLD

Elizabeth Chamberlayne Hadas (1915–92) was a teacher, a reader, a translator, a mother. Those activities were not separate parts of her life. She was the most bookish person I have ever known. She read aloud to my sister and me long before we could possibly understand what she was reading to us, and it is not an accident that both of us have devoted our lives to books, one of us as an author and the other as a publisher. She and our father read *The Story of Ferdinand* aloud to us over and over. It was one of those books that parents could enjoy as much as children did, which doubtless accounts for its long life and vast popularity.

Elizabeth Hadas was brought up to teach. Her father, Lewis Chamberlayne, a professor of classics, died when she was a very small child. Faced with raising two daughters, her mother, Bessie, took a job teaching at St. Catherine's School in Richmond, Virginia. Bessie and her little girls lived on campus, presumably in exchange for supervising the boarding students. From St. Catherine's, Elizabeth went to Bryn Mawr, and after graduation she went on to teach Latin at St. Timothy's School. Eventually she developed an interest in seeing the world beyond girls' schools. She moved to New York during the war years, married Moses Hadas, had two daughters, and stayed at home with us until 1959, when she went back to teaching Latin at Spence, another girls' school. She spent the rest of her career there.

It was through her teaching at Spence that she came to translate *Ferdinand.* The mother of one of her students was an editor at the David McKay

Company who, as many other publishers were probably doing in the early 1960s, was looking for a book that could duplicate the recent astonishing success of *Winnie Ille Pu*. She thought of *Ferdinand*, and she thought of her daughter's Latin teacher as a translator. Like *Winnie the Pooh*, *Ferdinand* was extremely popular and had very recognizable illustrations. It goes without saying that *Ferdinandus* did not sell as well as *Winnie Ille Pu*. Attempts to duplicate that kind of completely improbable success never work. But the vogue for translation at that time was strong enough to inspire Elizabeth Hadas to translate a few of Aesop's fables into Latin, though these translations were never published.

My sister Rachel writes movingly in her postscript about the theme of mothering that we all remember from *Ferdinand*, and she has written equally movingly elsewhere about the value of reading aloud to children. Like hers, my early memories are built of stories read aloud by my parents—my mother patiently reading favorites like *The Story About Ping* and *Boppit, Please Stop It* over and over as mothers so often must, my father reading *Alice in Wonderland* and *Just-So Stories*, editing and even embellishing them with his own jokes as he went along. My mother taught me to read, and I knew I had learned when I was able to read *Little House in the Big Woods* aloud to her one chapter at a time while she cooked dinner and I sat on a stool in the kitchen.

In bookish families like ours, reading aloud is not just a major component of parenting—even in adulthood it remains an important way to express affection. On long car trips we don't listen to books on tape; we read to each other. Our family is not only bookish and given to reading aloud but is also a hotbed of translation. As Rachel suggests, Elizabeth had help from Moses, a prolific translator from several languages, and Rachel has carried the tradition on.

There is something very intimate about Elizabeth's use of Latin in her dedication of *Ferdinandus* to Moses, perhaps because it seems to encode their courtship, when she was his student. And translation can express other kinds of love. When parents read to small children they are translating the vast world into a story and into a language that the children can understand. They make the world safe for us in just the way Rachel describes our mother's style of parenting: "to be her child was to be taken care of." My friend Paul Skenazy makes this point when he tells a story about his son Jason at the age of two picking up a favorite book. Paul asked him, "What does it say?" Pretending to read, Jason replied, "I . . . love . . . you."

—Beth Hadas

About the Author

Munro Leaf first achieved literary success with the children's book *Grammar Can Be Fun*, which was followed by others in the same series, including *Manners Can Be Fun*. His most widely known and beloved work, however, is *The Story of Ferdinand*, which was composed in less than an hour for his friend, the illustrator Robert Lawson. It has been translated into more than 60 languages, and was said to be Ghandi's favorite book. Munro Leaf died in 1976 at the age of 71.

About the Illustrator

Robert Lawson illustrated his first book, *The Wee Men of Ballywooden* by Arthur Mason, in 1930, following years of work as a commercial illustrator. Born in New York City and a graduate of the New York School of Fine and Applied Arts (Parsons), where he won several scholarships for line drawing and illustration, he is the only person to receive both the Newbery and Caldecott Medals. He is best known for *The Story of Ferdinand*, but was also a successful author, most notably of *Ben and Me* (1939), which he also illustrated. Robert Lawson died in 1957.

About the Typefaces

The Latin text of *Ferdinandus Taurus* has been set in Monotype Van Dijck, a lively sixteenth-century Dutch face originally cut by Christoffel van Dyck, a resident of Amsterdam and an exact contemporary of Rembrandt. After the death of Christoffel, the foundry passed to his son, Abraham, and after his death in 1673 the punches and matrices were auctioned off to Daniel Elzevier, the famous Amsterdam printer and bookseller. Eventually, the entire stock found its way to the celebrated Enschedé Typefoundry at Haarlem.

The glossary and postscripts have been set in Adobe Caslon. Designed and cut by William Caslon in the 1720s and 1730s, they have been copied and reinterpreted for over two centuries, their unrivaled success due to the exceptional readability of the type. The present version, designed directly in the digital medium and modeled on the letters cut by Caslon (rather than on later interpretations for letterpress or photo-typesetting), was created for Adobe Systems by Carol Twombly.

The publishers wish to extend special thanks to the Pierpont Morgan Library, the repository of Robert Lawson's archive, for providing reproduction transparencies from the original drawings, and to Dean Bornstein for his care in overseeing the design and production of the book.

The book has been designed and typeset by Dean Bornstein